The Sandman and the Turtles

MICHAEL MORPURGO

EGMONT

For Lula Léa.

EGMONT
We bring stories to life

First published in Great Britain in 1991 by William Heinmann Ltd
This edition published 2006 by Egmont UK Limited
239 Kensington High Street, London W8 6SA

Text Copyright © 1991 Michael Morpurgo
Cover illustration copyright © 2006 Chris Inns
Inside illustration copyright © 1991 Els van Egeraat

The moral rights of the author and cover illustrator have been asserted

ISBN 978 1 4052 2667 7
ISBN 1 4052 2667 6

3 5 7 9 10 8 6 4 2

A CIP catalogue record for this title is available from the British Library

Printed and bound in Great Britain by the CPI Group

CHAPTER ONE

YOU CAN KEEP CHRISTMASSES, BIRTHDAYS and all that. For me the high time of the year was always my summer holidays at Treginnis Isaf, Uncle Rob's and Aunty Eleri's farm down by the sea in Wales. It was a place of clambering rocks, ratty barns and fields of shifting sheep and uddery cows. You could pick up the warm eggs, you could clean down the milking parlour. And all around were the cliffs and beaches where we basked and swam with the seals, where we watched killer-whales and porpoises. For a city boy like me it was a paradise, and I never wanted anything better. Nothing could have been better. You could lean against the wind on Buzzard Rock, you could loll laughing in the fields, fly Barry's yellow kite, or race his battered boats across the duck pond. Every year was the best, but best of all was the summer of the Sandman, the giant turtles – and the great grey cucumber.

I arrived as usual by train and Aunty Eleri was there to pick me up, all smiles and kisses and smelling of milk. But no Barry. I soon found out why.

'Only happened yesterday morning,' she said, fighting with the gear lever. 'Playing football he was in that top field with his da, you know the rocky field beyond the sheep-dip pit? Tripped and broke his leg in two places. Nasty. Plastered he is all the way up, and he's got six stitches in his head. Blood all over the place. Concussion maybe. We've got to keep him quiet for a couple of days.' She patted my knee. 'There we are then. You're here now. That'll cheer him up.'

It was a blow. Barry was my cousin of course, but he was also my best friend in all the world. Like two sides of a coin we were, but as different as chalk and cheese. Barry was a head taller than me, ran faster and knew where and how to catch fish. He could sweeten up a fox just by whistling through his throat like a screaming rabbit; and no one played practical jokes like Barry, no one. As for me, I read a lot of books, played chess like a Russian Master and could say the alphabet backwards in less than four seconds flat. Aunty Eleri talked all the way back to the farm, but I never heard a word. I was wondering what I was going to do with myself for the whole month with Barry's leg in plaster. 'There we are now,' she said. 'We're home.'

Polly came skipping out to the car as we pulled up outside the house. Polly was Barry's little sister. Only seven years old she was and bouncy like a puppy. She was maybe a little bigger than the year before, but not much; and I noticed she was missing her two top front teeth. She took my hand at once and dragged me off. 'Barry's busted his leg,' she said cheerfully.

Barry was propped up on the sitting-room sofa in his pyjamas. His great white leg seemed twice as long as the other one and twice as fat too. He wiggled his chalky toes at me. 'Hello, Mike,' he said, grinning. 'I've bust my leg.' And he patted the plaster.

'So I see,' I said.

'Da's fault,' he went on. 'He tripped me.'

'He never,' Polly said. I won't tell you what Barry said, but I felt at home already.

Tea-time brought Uncle Rob and Dadci in

from the fields and Aunty Eleri had made a tea of Welsh cakes and scones and raspberry jam and cream. I never liked the first meal though. I suppose I always felt a bit awkward. They all kept asking me questions about Mum, about school, except Dadci – that's my grandfather – who just smiled at me and pushed the cream closer. 'Eat up now Michael, there's a good boy,' he said. 'We'll fatten you up if it's the last thing we do.'

Later it was Polly's bath-time and she came down in her primrose dressing-gown with the blue butterflies. All pink and clean she was, and she said she'd have her story now.

'What about a "please" then?' said Dadci frowning at her.

'Please,' said Polly sweetly. Dadci was about the only one who could make her behave.

Stories at Treginnis were like a long happy sigh at the end of each day. You sat on Dadci's lap in the deep brown armchair with the stuffing coming out of the arms; and he'd always begin: 'Let me see now . . .' Of course I was too old to sit on his lap – it was Polly's turn these days – but I listened just the same. Everyone did. We all knew every word, every sentence of every story; but you never tired of them because he told them like he was telling them for the first time, like they were really true, and you could join in whenever you liked.

We were all there that evening when Dadci began with the story of the Sandman, all about those rocks down on Whitesands Beach that looked like a great fat giant lying asleep in the sand. (So we all snored noisily.) 'He fell asleep there thousands and thousands of years ago after a terrible storm-tossed journey across from Ireland in a huge coracle pulled by three giant turtles. Now there's not many who know

this, children, but if you stay still in one place for long enough you turn into rock. True now.' (And we all froze stiff where we were.) 'And that's just what happened to the Sandman and the three giant turtles. They turned into the three Turtle Rocks out in the bay. And his huge great coracle, the one that was wrecked in the storm, well, we all know what became of that, don't we?' (And we all nodded and chorused: 'Coracle Island!') Dadci went on. 'They've none of them moved a muscle in thousands of years. And that's how they'll stay until the Sandman wakes up; and just as soon as he wakes up – and one day he will – he'll want to go back home to Ireland where he belongs. Fair play. But the thing is, children, he'll only wake up when he feels someone loves him enough to feed him and look after him and help him home to Ireland.'

'I will,' said Polly.

'Course you will,' Dadci said, and he laughed and lit his pipe.

'Another one, another one,' said Polly, wafting away the smoke. An old trick this – I'd done it myself. You talk Dadci into another story and another story and another story so you never have to go to bed. It wasn't that difficult either because Dadci loved telling his stories. He'd settle back, puff his pipe, and off he'd go again.

Next he told us the one about the lighthouse on Coracle Island and the lighthouse keeper, an old Russian sea captain called, (and we all chanted his name together) 'Sergei Ivanovitch Prokoviev!' 'On a dark and dreadful night over a hundred years ago Sergei Ivanovitch Prokoviev, captain of the fastest clipper in the Russian merchant fleet, was caught in a hurricane and driven on to Coracle Rock. He lost his ship and most of his crew with it. It wasn't his fault but he blamed himself just the same, and it was the shame of it that kept him from going home to Russia. Instead he stayed and became the lighthouse keeper on Coracle Rock, and every night without fail the light shone out from the lighthouse to warn away the ships. Then one night the light never came on; and when they went to find out what the matter was, he had disappeared. They found the door locked fast from the inside. They had to pick the lock. Inside it was all shipshape, the bed made, the washing-up done, and just one window left open. And on the table they found an empty cake tin – Welsh cakes were his favourite – and a sky-blue teapot. And there was more. On the chest of drawers was a clock that had stopped at precisely five o'clock, and a bottle of vodka with an empty glass beside it. They found his clothes folded neatly on the top of an old sea chest and gull's feathers by the window. Can't be a shadow of doubt about it, children, old Sergei had turned himself into a seagull so's he could fly home at last to Russia. And there's some say,' Dadci was finishing in a foggy flurry of pipe smoke, 'that if you were to put the light going again in the lighthouse, then that would bring old Sergei . . .' (and we all chorused again: 'Ivanovitch Prokoviev!') 'back to his lighthouse so's he could cook himself some more Welsh cakes and pour himself a nice cup of tea.'

'Shivery,' said Polly, and please could she have the dragon story now? 'Please, Dadci,' she pleaded. 'I want the one about the spikey blood-red dragon that sleeps on his treasure in the damp dark lair down on Whaletooth Beach. I like it when all the little people come creeping, creeping across the pebbles to steal his treasure and he hears the stones crunching and it wakes him up and he chases them, and they run away fast as they can and he breathes out his fire and his thick black smoke and he frizzles them up so's they're all turned into the standing stones up on Buzzard Rock. Tell us that one. Please, Dadci.'

'But, Polly, there's nothing much left to tell now, is there?' said Dadci laughing. 'You've just gone and told it all yourself, haven't you?'

'There we are then,' said Aunty Eleri, seizing her opportunity. 'Say goodnight now, Polly.'

'Cooked your goose there,' Barry sniggered.

'Dumbo!' said Polly, and then she had to go. If there was one thing Uncle Rob could not stand it was arguments.

Barry and I lay in the dark and chatted way into the night. We had a whole year to catch up on. With just a little bit of sleep in between, we were still at it at breakfast when Polly announced that she would be going to the beach.

'Not on your own you're not,' said Aunty Eleri. And Polly looked across the table at me with the smile of a tyrant.

'He's busy,' said Barry firmly.

'Pegleg!' said Polly.

'Parrot,' said Barry.

'That'll be enough of that,' Uncle Rob growled from behind his newspaper. As usual it was Aunty Eleri who kept the peace and sorted it all out. I would be shared: I'd spend the mornings (if that was all right with me) with Polly down on the beach, and the afternoons with Barry. Barry was none too happy about it, but he perked up when I said we could maybe fly his kite that afternoon if the wind was right.

So there I was then, tripping down through the fields to Whitesands Beach with Polly leading me like a donkey. And like a donkey it was me who carried the bucket, the spade, the towels and the picnic.

Polly had grown up a lot. She told me so all the way there, and then opened her mouth and waggled a wobbly tooth at me just to prove it. She fell on her knees in the sand beside the Sandman Rocks and clasped her hands together. 'I know,' she said, beaming up at me. 'Let's pretend we're children. We'll build a real Sandman all of our own and we'll make him fat as fat can be. You make his body, and I'll find some shells to make his buttons and his mouth and his eyes and his nose. Come on.'

There are some people who just expect you to do what you're told, and Polly was one of them. So I didn't argue. Off she went down the beach, bottom in the air, looking for cowries and mussels and cockles and limpets, while I began to think about how to build the Sandman's body. It was going to take a lot of digging and an awful lot of sand. As Dadci said in his story, the Sandman was enormous, a huge sleeping giant stretching at least four metres from the round rock that was his head to the two sticking-up rocks that made up his feet. One rocky knee was raised up and bent, and one of his arms looked as if it was pointing out to sea, out towards the three Turtle Rocks.

I began with the arms. I always do the easiest things first. I'm like that. I wasn't going to have to do too much fetching and carrying to flesh out the arms. The sand was still wet from the tide, heavy to carry but all the better for sculpting and shaping. Polly would come back from time to time to show me her collection of shells and to tell me just what she thought of my handiwork. 'Fatter,' she kept saying. 'He's got to be a great fat giant like Dadci says.' So all that morning I made him fatter. By the time I'd finished, he had a huge great belly like a sumo wrestler and he had arms and legs to match. Polly added the finishing touches – cuttle shells for his mouth and his eyebrows, clams for his ears, cockleshells for his teeth and cowries for his fingernails and toenails, limpet shells for his eyes and a huge black oyster shell for his nose; mussels for buttons, sea lettuce for his hair and a great big belt of seaweed around his tummy with a crab shell for a buckle. She stood beside me and looked down at him critically.

'But don't you think he should be a little fatter?' she said, her head on one side.

'No,' I said quickly. 'I think he's just right as he is. Anyway, there's no point; the tide'll soon be in and he'll be all washed away.'

I shouldn't have said that.

'Oh no!' she cried and ran down to the sea. I followed her. 'You're got to stop it, Mikey. You've got to stop the sea coming in,' she said, and I laughed – well, you would, wouldn't you? 'It's not funny,' she shouted, stamping her foot. 'You've got to stop it, else he'll drown.' And a little wave ran up the beach and over her toes. 'Quick!' she cried and she grabbed my arm and tugged on it hard.

'But there's nothing we can do,' I said. 'It's the moon.'

'The moon?' She was screaming at me now. 'What's the daft moon got to do with it?'

'A lot,' I said, and I began to explain as patiently as I could all about how it was the pull of the moon that made the tides rise and fall like they did, and that there really wasn't much I could do about it.

'Stuff the moon,' she said, and she fetched her spade and began to dig furiously in the sand between the Sandman's feet and the rising tide.

'What are you doing?' I asked her. Ask a silly question.

'S'obvious,' she said. 'If we dig a big, big

hole, then the sea will all fall in and the Sandman won't get drowned will he?' I tried to tell her you couldn't dig a hole big enough, that there was quite a lot of sea out there and it was all coming our way. But she wouldn't listen.

So side by side we dug together, and every time I looked up the sea was coming in closer. Then it was trickling into our hole and there was a sandy pool at the bottom of it. 'See?' Polly was jumping up and down in triumph. 'I told you, didn't I?' Sometimes with some people it's best not to argue. I stood and I waited and I watched as the tide filled the hole, overflowed, and then spread slowly up the beach. Polly shouted at it to go back, but had no more success than King Canute had had before her. In spite of all her fury it lapped over her feet and rolled on up towards the Sandman.

'You can always make another one,' I said.

There wasn't much else I could say.

'But he's my Sandman, and I don't want him to drown.' And then she began to cry. She was standing by the Sandman's feet now and the tears were running down into her mouth. I put my arm around her.

'We'll make you another one just the same,' I said. 'Tomorrow, I promise.'

'But I don't want one just the same, I want him.' A whispering ripple of sea ran up over the sand and touched the Sandman's ankle. 'Oh wake up, Mr Sandman,' Polly cried. 'Please wake up. Please. We got to wake him up. We got to.' And she crouched down and bellowed in his ear. 'Wake up, Mr Sandman. Wake up!' She turned to me with pleading eyes. 'Oh help me, Mikey, please help me.' And so I found myself shouting with her. I took hold of his rocky knee. I even tried to shake it. He didn't move. The sea came hissing up the beach and washed around his other foot.

And then quite suddenly I remembered Dadci's story. 'Maybe if you told him you loved him, that you'd look after him, you know like Dadci said. Tell him you'll feed him,' I said. 'We've got the picnic, haven't we?'

She looked at me for just a moment and then she put her arms around his neck, kissed him on his sandy cheek and whispered in his clamshell ear: 'We got crisps, Mr Sandman. We got tomatoes. We got peanut-butter sandwiches and hard-boiled eggs. And I do love you, Mr Sandman and I'll feed you and look after you for always and always, and I'll help you get back to Ireland if you want, honest I will.' And she kissed him again on both cheeks and then wiped the sand off her mouth.

A finger twitched, then a hand and then an arm. It could have been the wind whipping at the sand, but I knew it wasn't. The limpet-shell

eyes opened and blinked and squinted at the sunlight. Polly sprang off him and backed away towards me as the Sandman propped himself up on his elbows. He looked us up and down. I don't think he could believe what he was seeing, and he wasn't the only one. He lifted a sandy arm and rubbed his eyes with the back of his wrist. When he yawned I felt Polly's hand creep into mine, and when he sat up I realised she was biting my knuckles.

Just sitting up the Sandman was as tall as Uncle Rob – and Uncle Rob's tall enough. And then he breathed in deeply and stretched and yawned again and scratched his head. When he'd finished he twiddled his finger in his ear. I kept expecting everything to fall off, the sand or the seaweed or the shells, but not a single thing did, not a grain of sand, nothing. Under his mop of sea-lettuce hair his face was round like a pumpkin, and when he stood up and smiled down at us his cockleshell teeth gleamed white in the sun. 'Best sleep I've had in a long time,' he said. He spoke in a deep echoing drawl of a voice that sounded as if he was still yawning. 'Was I dreaming or was I not?' he went on. 'Did someone say something about a bite to eat?' And he patted his belly in a meaningful sort of a way. He was so tall it hurt your neck to look up at him. I'm telling you he was a giant, a living, breathing giant.

Polly wasn't going to be able to reply, not with her teeth deep into my knuckles, so I thought I'd better say something myself. 'We've got some sausage rolls,' I said.

CHAPTER TWO

HE LIKED THE SAUSAGE ROLLS – ALL OF them. He liked the peanut-butter sandwiches, the tomatoes and the boiled eggs – shells and all. Then he ate the crisps, Polly's cheese-and-onion and my salt-and-vinegar. He ate the packets too. I think he liked my salt-and-vinegar best because he burped loud and long when he'd finished. Polly smiled at that and he winked at her. The orange juice went down in one gulp and then he sat back against a rock and wiped his mouth with the back of his hand. 'That's better,' he said. 'I'm more me old self again now.' And then his brow furrowed as he looked past us out to sea. 'Will you look at that now: me poor old coracle quite upside-downed. I made it all by meself, so I did. I showed 'em. I showed 'em. You'll never float in that they said. Watch me, I said. Just watch me. And I did it just like I said I would, all the way here by coracle. And then, well, I had a little bit of an accident, that's all. I'm not making excuses, but it was all down to me empty stomach. You see, I hadn't brought quite enough food along for the ride – sure I didn't know how far it would be. And I can't be doing without me food – sends me right off to the Land of Nod. I can't help meself. Last thing I remember we was rolling about in a terrible awful gale and I was yawning me head off and me tummy was rumbling louder than the very thunder itself. Then me poor old coracle was turned upside down and I was in the water, and me darlin' turtles were bobbing about me all seasick.' Suddenly he jumped to his feet. 'Me turtles! Me turtles! That's them out there. You don't see them? Rock solid they are by the look of them. Well I'll soon sort that out.' And he stuck his fingers in his mouth and whistled. 'Will you wake up you dozy boys! Wake up now!' And he whistled again, louder this time.

First one turtle lifted its head out of the sea and then another and another, and I'm telling you, not a word of a lie, the three Turtle Rocks began to glide towards us through the water. Polly and I, we just stood and gaped as the giant turtles rode through the surf and flippered up across the tide-ribbed sand. The Sandman bent down and patted each of them on the head. 'Am I glad to see you!' he said. 'Didn't I tell you we'd get here? Didn't I tell you? And we did, didn't we? Now all we've got to do is get ourselves back home where we belong, but that's not going to be so easy, not without me coracle. Turned turtle it did, if you see what I'm saying.' And I swear the turtles smiled. 'And will you just look what they've gone and done to me lovely coracle. They've only gone and built a lighthouse on it, that's all.' And he shook his head and sighed. 'Still, something'll turn up. Like me two little friends here, waking me up after all these years and looking after me like I was a brother. Darlin' they are, darlin'.' His tummy gurgled like an orchestra tuning up, and he grinned down at us. 'Would you believe it? I'm still hungry, and me poor old turtles will be starved half to death. We'll be needing a little something from time to time, won't we, boys? Can you help us out I wonder?'

'Course we can,' I said. The Sandman reached down and lifted us up so that we were each sat in the crook of his arm.

'Aren't I just the lucky Sandman,' he laughed. 'Bladderwrack sandwiches and milk. Can you manage that? And we all love milk, don't we, boys? Drink it till the cows come home.' And he shook so much when he laughed that I was quite sure some of the sand would fall off, but none of it did. 'We'll find the bladderwrack for ourselves, but maybe you'll take care of the bread and the milk.'

'All right,' I said, 'we'll do our best.'

He set us down again on the sand and we ran off up the cliff path. When we looked back, the Sandman was crouched down and talking to his turtles. 'What's bladderwrack?' I asked.

'Seaweed, dumbo,' Polly said – she always had a nice way with words did Polly – and we ran on home.

I knew you couldn't tell Polly anything, but I tried just the same. 'Best not to say a word,' I said. 'They won't believe you, not in a million years they won't.'

We met Dadci sitting in a deckchair in the back garden, his straw hat over his face. She ran right up to him and shook him awake. 'We seen him, Dadci. We seen him,' she said.

He was smiling patiently as he lifted his hat off his face. 'Who's that?' he said.

'The Sandman,' said Polly. 'And he's just like you said he'd be. He woke up, and we gave him all our sausage rolls and things. He ate everything, didn't he, Mikey?'

Dadci smiled. 'What, everything?' he said. 'Well now, and how tall was he? Was he as tall as your da?'

Polly stood on tiptoe and reached up as high as she could. 'Course he was,' she said. 'He was huge as huge, 'bout as high as you and Da stood on top of each other. Honest.' Dadci winked at me as Aunty Eleri came out into the garden with Barry behind her on his crutches.

'It seems like they've had quite a morning,' said Dadci. 'They woke up the Sandman and he ate their picnic.' Barry laughed out loud.

'He did too, pegleg,' Polly protested indignantly. Then she turned to me. 'Didn't he, Mikey?' I smiled weakly and shrugged my shoulders. I wished she wouldn't call me 'Mikey'.

'Course,' I said. Well, what else could I say?

'See?' said Polly, and I could tell Barry was more than a little disappointed in me. I was in a spot here. I mean I didn't want to upset anyone, not Polly, not Barry, not anyone.

Polly went on: 'And then he just whistled and the Three Turtles came swimming up out of the sea and he says he wants to go home, but he can't because his coracle's turned upside down and someone's put a lighthouse on top of it, and he eats bladderwrack sandwiches and milk – honest he does. It's just like you said in the story, Dadci.'

'And why wouldn't it be?' said Dadci chortling wickedly. 'I ask you, would I tell you a fib? Would I now?'

'I'm starved,' said Polly.

'Of course you are,' said Aunty Eleri. 'What do you expect if you go giving your picnic to the Sandman like that. I'm not surprised you're hungry. Greedy old Sandman.' She turned to me with a knowing, confidential look in her eyes. 'And what about you Michael? You look a bit peaky.'

If I did look peaky, it wasn't because I was hungry.

'Too much Polly,' said Barry.

'Pegleg! Dumbo!' said Polly, and she stuck her tongue out at him, and then ran indoors after Aunty Eleri, still rabbiting on about the Sandman.

'Come on,' said Barry. 'I've got the kite ready and the wind's just right.'

'You go careful,' said Dadci. 'Don't go prancing around on that leg of yours.' And then Polly came running out again.

'What about the Sandman's supper?' she said.

'The Sandman can sing for his supper,' Barry said. 'Mike's flying my kite.'

'Later,' I said to Polly. 'We'll do it later.' It wasn't at all easy keeping everyone happy.

'My sister's a nutter,' said Barry as we walked away, 'a real little nutter.' And then he let me have a go with one of his crutches. 'We'll have a crutch race,' he said, and I discovered he could still run faster than me even with a broken leg.

That afternoon I flew the yellow kite from the back garden and it soared up over the fields around Buzzard Rock. And Barry was right – it was perfect kite-flying weather, the breeze off the sea filling the kite with a life of its own. It was a wheeling buzzard, a rearing cobra, a skimming swallow, whatever it wanted to be. I didn't seem to be able to control it at all. When the kite decided it would dive-bomb the cows and scatter them in all directions, Barry took it off me and flew it himself. And after that, whenever it grounded in the rocks or the gorse, I was sent off to retrieve it and launch it again. I didn't mind a bit. I was with Barry and I could watch a kite for ever. He obviously didn't believe a word Polly had said because he never mentioned Polly or the Sandman all afternoon, and neither did I. When Aunty Eleri called him inside to lie down for a bit to rest his leg, I went off to help Uncle Rob with the evening milking.

We'd just put the cows out and I was washing down the parlour with the hosepipe when Polly appeared carrying a churn in one hand and a plastic bag in the other. 'What you got there?' said Uncle Rob taking off his milking apron.

'Bread for the Sandman,' she said, 'and Dadci gave me some crusts too for the turtles – he says turtles like their crusts better if they've been soaked in milk.'

'Well, if anyone knows what turtles like,' said Uncle Rob, winking at me, 'then it'll be Dadci.' And he patted her on the head as he passed. 'I'll leave you to finish up then,

Michael. I'm going to have a word with Barry – frightened the cows silly he did, him and that flipping kite of his. All upset and messy, they were.' I kept very quiet. I'm not at all brave when it comes to owning up, I never have been.

Polly waited until he was gone and then handed me the churn. 'You do it,' she said. 'I can't reach, and anyway I'm not allowed. Full to the top, mind. Remember there's three of them and the Sandman.' So I did what I was told, dipped the scoop in the tank and filled the churn right up. 'We got to hurry,' she said. 'Mum wouldn't let me go down to the beach without you. I told her the Sandman would look after me, but she still said I had to wait for you. Come on, he'll be waiting.'

We spotted the Sandman from the cliff path. He was out at sea, sitting astride one of the giant turtles. The other two were swimming

alongside. When he saw us coming he waved
and the turtles turned and made for the beach.
We ran down to meet him. Polly was holding
up the plastic bag. 'We got lots of bread for
your sandwiches and we got crusts too, for the
turtles,' she said. 'Dadci said they like crusts.'

'And so they do,' said the Sandman. 'Aren't
you the clever ones! Let me see now . . .' He
sounded just like Dadci about to begin one of

his stories. 'Let me see now . . .' He was looking all around him on the beach – I had no idea what for – but then he found it, a great saucer-shaped rock that lay tipped sideways in the sand right under the cliff. 'This'll maybe do,' he said as he inspected it carefully. Then he took a deep breath, bent his knees, spread his arms out wide and lifted it, just like that.

'What're you doing?' said Polly.

'I suppose you could say I'm sort of laying the table,' the Sandman said, 'for me turtles. In the sea there's not a creature that swims better, but they're just not made for walking on the land. It hurts their flippers, so it does.' No huffing, no puffing, easy as you like, he carried the rock all the way back down the beach and dropped it in the sand near the sea.

Polly poured in the milk and broke up the crusts – she wouldn't let me do it. She sprinkled them on the milk; and then we mixed them round and round until they were well and truly soaked.

'There we are then,' he said – now he sounded like Aunty Eleri – and he licked his fingers. 'Dinner is served, boys. Bread crusts all nice and soggy, just like you like them. Come and get it.' And the turtles scooped their way out of the shallows, lifted their wizened heads over the lip of the rock and dipped their chins in the milk. Eyes closed in bliss, they lapped and chomped and licked until the rock was quite dry. This all took some time because, of course, turtles do everything in slow motion. Meanwhile the Sandman was busy scoffing his sandwiches. He ate with his mouth open, the bladderwrack popping and crunching as he chewed. When he'd finished he washed it all down with what was left of the milk from the churn. Then he burped, loud and long, and loosened the seaweed belt around his belly.

'Have you ever had bladderwrack sandwiches?' he asked. We shook our heads. 'Sure it's the best brain food in the whole world. It helps you with your thinking processes – well that was what me old mother told me and she was more than usually right.' He shook his head sadly. 'But I've been thinking and thinking, and I've still no notion how I'm going to get meself back home to Ireland. I thought maybe I could ride back on me turtles – take turns maybe – but it's no good, no good at all. We've tried it. They're not as young as they were. They can just about carry me as far as me poor old upside-downed coracle out there, but they'd never get me all the way back to Ireland.'

Polly wasn't listening. She was shielding her eyes with her arm as she looked out towards the lighthouse. I knew what she was thinking because I was thinking just the same thing.

'Please, Mr Sandman,' she said, 'can you take us over there, over to Coracle Island? No one's been over there, not since Sergei whatshisname turned himself into a seagull and flew off home to Russia – that's what Dadci said. Oh please! We could ride on the turtles.'

The Sandman thought for a moment. 'Indeed we could,' he said, 'indeed we could. It's not that far and I don't suppose they'd mind, not one bit, not after all you've done for us. And when all's said and done, one good turn deserves another, does it not? When do you want to go?'

'Now,' said Polly, smiling through her gappy teeth.

'Well,' said the Sandman to the turtles, 'you heard the little lady. Let's go.'

And so off we went, riding the turtles over the waves towards the lighthouse on Coracle Island, and me clinging on for dear life to the shell so that I didn't fall off. It was like riding a horse without stirrups – not that I've ever done it, but you know what I mean. You cling on and you hope. The turtle's shell wasn't shell at all, but leathery and slimy, and I kept slipping and sliding. But what worried me most was the thought that at any moment my turtle might decide to dive and swim on underwater. I was grinning with terror, doing my very best not to look frightened. Polly looked across at me laughing and shrieking with delight. 'Gee up!' she cried. 'Gee up!' And the three of us ploughed through the sea, the Sandman's turtle a good deal lower in the water than ours – as you might expect.

It wasn't a race, but I was pleased nonetheless when I found myself out in front, though less pleased when I saw the mountainous waves crashing over the rocks on Coracle Island. I wanted to turn back but

I didn't know how. I clenched my teeth, took a deep breath and gripped the shell even harder, but my fingers were numb with cold now and seemed to have no strength left in them. One wrong wave and I'd be in the sea. I needn't have worried though. The turtle waited for just the perfect wave and we were carried in over the raging surf and washed up safe and sound on a narrow, pebbly beach. I got off, patted his shell and tried to stop my knees shaking. 'Thanks,' I said. And the turtle blinked his black eyes at me as if to say that it was no trouble, no trouble at all.

As soon as the other two joined me on the beach, we began the long climb up to the lighthouse. Every now and again the Sandman would stop and sigh. 'Me poor old coracle, all bashed about and upside-downed. It's not fair, it's not fair at all.' Polly was clambering on ahead like a goat. She arrived at the door of the lighthouse first and tried to shake it open, but she couldn't budge it. I tried once, but it was locked.

'Do you want to go inside then?' the Sandman asked, and he turned the handle. When it didn't open, he put his foot against the door and pushed it. The lock broke at once. 'There we are,' he said. 'Easily done. I'd go with you, but I don't think I'd ever get myself through the little door would I?' And he was right about that. So Polly and I went alone into the cold dark of the lighthouse.

In front of us was a winding stairway.

'You go first,' Polly whispered.

'Why are you whispering?' I whispered.

'In case he's still here, you know, Sergei Ivanovitch thingamyjig. Maybe he's still here.'

I very much hoped he wasn't.

The steps were steep and narrow and my legs began aching almost at once. Eighty-five steps I counted, until we came at last into a large round room with a table in the middle of it and a chair. There was nothing on the table except a teapot and a tin. Polly opened the tin. 'His Welsh cake tin and it's empty,' she whispered. I took the lid off the teapot. There were just a few dry tea-leaves inside.

The clock on the chest of drawers had stopped at precisely five o'clock, and beside it was an empty glass and a bottle of something. I could just read the writing on the label. 'It's vodka, isn't it?' said Polly. And it was.

All around the walls were pictures of sailing ships, but when I looked closer I saw that each one was of the same ship; and on every ledge stood an intricate, detailed matchstick model of a ship, all different sizes, but they were all the same ship, the same as the one in the pictures. And above the neatly made-up bed was a faded photo of a bearded sailor and his wife. 'That's him,' I said. 'That's Sergei Ivanovitch Prokofiev.

Must be.' Then Polly was tugging at my shirt and I looked around. There was a chest against the wall and a blue uniform with gold buttons laid out neatly on top of it. On the floor beside it was a pair of black boots. But Polly was still pulling at me and pointing. She was pointing at the window and the window was open just as Dadci had always said it was, and there below it were a few white feathers on the floor. Seagull's feathers. Polly's cold hand crept into mine. 'Shivery,' she said.

CHAPTER THREE

IT WAS A LONG WAY DOWN. I WAS LOOKING out of the window at the sea seething around rocks below. The Sandman was sitting with his turtles and twiddling his finger in his ear; and back on land I could see Uncle Rob out on his tractor with the seagulls flying all about him. Polly was calling me. 'Mikey! Mikey! Quick, come and look at this.' When I turned round she was nowhere to be seen. 'I'm up here,' she said from somewhere up above me. And then I saw the ladder and the trap-door in the ceiling. I climbed up into a smaller room with a domed glass roof and windows all around, and in the middle of it stood a great lamp twice as high as Polly, who was standing beside it, her eyes bright with excitement.

'We could light it,' she said.

'You can't,' I said.

'I can,' said Polly, and I could see she meant it. 'I got matches.' And she had too. 'I found them in the drawer of that table over there, and there's oil in those cans too, lots of it. All we got to do is pour it in and light it up. Simple. Only I can't lift the cans – too heavy for me. But you could.' I turned away. I didn't want to stay, not any more. It was like walking on someone's grave. 'Oh come on, Mikey, please,' she said. 'Everything else Dadci told us has come true, hasn't it? We only got to light the lamp and it'll bring old Sergei whatdyoucallhim back for his tea and his Welsh cakes, just like he said. You'll see.'

I didn't much like the idea of bringing Sergei Ivanovitch Prokofiev back from the dead, yet I was just a little tempted. 'Please, Mikey. Please.' She was holding out the matches. 'I'll let you light it,' she said, wheedling expertly. So I was persuaded, conned, bullied, call it what you will.

It wasn't difficult to fill up the lamp. The first few matches must have been a bit damp and they refused to light, but at the fifth attempt the match caught and I touched it to the wick. The yellow fire ran around the wick and the heat of it forced us back. We stood and watched it, but it was so bright you couldn't look at it for long. 'That'll bring him back,' Polly said. 'I know it will.' But I wasn't quite so sure. I wasn't sure of anything, not any more.

All the way back, astride the turtles, we kept looking back and hoping for the first glimpse of Sergei's sailing ship hoving to round the headland. The return trip wasn't nearly so frightening, but just the same I was glad when it was over. We waited and watched together on the beach, but all we saw was the St David's lifeboat beating its way through a heavy swell out beyond Coracle Rock. The Sandman saw it too. 'Maybe I could borrow that one,' he said, 'just to get me home.' But Polly explained what the lifeboat was for.

'And anyway,' she went on, 'you'd have to bring it back again and so you'd be right back where you started from, wouldn't you?' All quite true of course.

The Sandman shrugged off his disappointment. 'No matter,' he said. 'Something'll turn up. It always does. Maybe I'll have to build me own coracle like I did before, but it takes for ever and it's a terrible lot of hard work.'

'We'll help you,' said Polly, 'won't we, Mikey?'

The Sandman smiled at us. 'You're darlin' little people,' he said, 'and I wouldn't want to be putting you to any more trouble; but if you could maybe bring us down some more bread for me bladderwrack sandwiches I'd love you for ever, so I would, and maybe a little milk for the boys too.' We turned to go. 'You won't forget now or we'll be all dropping off to sleep again and I've done enough of that for a lifetime.'

'We won't forget,' said Polly. And we left them on the beach and ran off up the cliff path.

On Buzzard Rock we stopped to look back out to sea. There was still no sailing ship. 'He'll come,' said Polly. 'He must come.' It was too light to be sure, but we both of us thought we could just make out our light up in the lighthouse glinting white against the red of the setting sun. Polly put her hands to her mouth and shouted. 'Come back Sergei

Ivanovitch . . .' and she looked to me for help.

'Prokofiev,' I said.

'Prokofiev,' she yelled. 'Come back!'

They were all there in the kitchen eating their supper by the time we got in.

'You've been a long time,' said Aunty Eleri. 'We started without you.' She wasn't angry. I've never seen Aunty Eleri angry, never.

'What've you two been up to?' said Uncle Rob. He shouldn't have asked.

Polly told them everything, all about the ride on the turtles, about the lighting of the lamp in the lighthouse, the lot. She ran to the window. 'Come and look,' she said. 'You can see for yourself.' Barry sniggered into his tomato soup and made a mess on the table.

Dadci turned to look out of the window. 'Well, I never,' he said. 'She's right you know.' And then Uncle Rob looked too.

'And you lit that all by yourself?' said Uncle Rob.

'With Mikey,' she said. 'Mikey helped me, didn't you, Mikey?' I nodded.

Barry leaned back in his chair and took one look out of the window. 'That's the sunset,' he scoffed. 'The lighthouse always looks like that when there's a sunset. Next thing you know, old Sergei Ivanovitch Prokofiev is going to walk right in here and ask for his tea and Welsh cakes.'

'You wait, pegleg,' said Polly fiercely. 'You just wait.'

Barry turned to me as I sat down beside him. 'So you've been turtle-surfing too, have you?' he said, licking the tomato soup off his lips and grinning provocatively.

'Course he has,' said Polly. 'You tell him, Mikey.'

'Good fun it was,' I said, and I smiled a smile

that I hoped would keep everyone happy; but Barry was looking from Polly to me and back again. I could see he wasn't sure what to think.

Supper was over and Polly demanded her stories as usual. She was careful to say 'please', and so she got her way. She sat on Dadci's lap, her thumb down her throat, her finger up her nose and she only took them out in order to interrupt. This she did frequently, telling everyone how the Sandman burped very loudly, how he was so strong he could pick up huge rocks just like they were beach balls and how if Sergei Ivanovitch Prokofiev looked anything like his picture then he'd have a great black beard and eyebrows that met in the middle. 'And now I want the dragon story,' she said, but by the time the spikey blood-red dragon came roaring out of his lair breathing fire on the little people and frizzling them all to stone, she was fast asleep.

Uncle Rob carried her up to bed, and when he came down again he said to Dadci: 'From now on I think she'd better tell you the stories. She talks about that Sandman just like she's met him.' I looked down at my feet because I didn't want anyone's eyes to catch mine.

'It's what's called imagination,' Aunty Eleri declared proudly. 'Maybe she'll write books when she grows up.'

'She can hardly write her name,' said Barry, and we went off to his room to play chess.

I let him beat me – and that was quite a sacrifice I can tell you – I don't like anyone beating me at chess. But I could tell he was fed up with being left on his own and even more fed up with Polly and her stories. He needed cheering up. Every now and again I'd steal a look out of the window at the lighthouse and every time I looked the light was that much brighter in the darkening sky,

and I wondered if anyone else would notice it.

Uncle Rob came in to see us before he went off to bed. He'd been out checking his cows. He always did that last thing at night. 'You two should be asleep,' he said, and then he nodded towards the window. 'Almost a full moon out there. If you didn't know better you'd think there was a light in Polly's lighthouse. Only the moon winking in the glass of course.' He went to the window; and then Dadci was at the bedroom door with our hot chocolates, one in each hand. 'To make you sleep,' he said as he put them down.

'Here, Da,' said Uncle Rob. 'Take a look at this. The moon's in the lighthouse again.' And Dadci leaned out of the window and took a deep breath.

'You're right,' he said. 'Twinkling away she is. Nights like this, they make you think anything could happen, anything at all.'

The hot chocolate didn't make us sleep. We lay there wide awake in the moonlit dark, but unlike the night before Barry said very little. He was thinking. I could feel it. I could feel that he knew that I knew something and was keeping it from him. More than once he sat up in bed and looked at the lighthouse and then across at me. He was trying to puzzle it all out.

'Polly's stories, all that stuff about the

Sandman and the lighthouse,' he said suddenly. 'She was having us on, wasn't she?'

'Not exactly,' I replied after a bit of thought. 'She just likes stories. She likes making them up, so they're true in a way, to her I mean.' I wanted to tell him, but I dared not. I knew he wouldn't believe me and I didn't want him to laugh at me. I didn't want him angry with me either. Maybe tomorrow, I thought. Yes, I'll tell him tomorrow.

'So they're not really true then?' he said.

'Course not, pegleg, dumbo,' I said, and he hit me with his pillow. I was glad that he couldn't see my face.

Outside in the farmyard a cockerel crowed noisily at the moon. I did not like myself at all. I lay awake most of that night promising myself that tomorrow I would tell everyone that Polly had not been telling stories. I would tell them no matter what, no matter how stupid it made me look. But come the morning I'd changed my mind again and decided I would take the easy way out. I would leave it to Sergei Ivanovitch Prokofiev. After all, if he did come back, then they'd have to believe everything – the Sandman, the lighthouse, everything.

When I came down to breakfast Barry wasn't looking at all happy. Polly was prattling on merrily. 'Barry's got to go to the doctor to have his stitches out,' she said. She knew how to niggle. Uncle Rob wasn't happy either because he had to take Barry in to the doctor's.

'Full of sick people in there,' he grumbled.

After they'd gone Polly took me straight down to the beach. She ran on ahead, leaving me, as usual, to carry everything, the milk churn, the bread for the Sandman and our picnic.

The sea that morning was a still blue pond that lapped listlessly against the rocks. There wasn't a whisper of wind. I scoured the sea for any sign of a sailing ship but both sea and sky were quite empty, except for one motionless tanker on the horizon. And so was the beach. No Sandman, no turtles.

'Where've they all gone?' Polly cried. 'And where's Sergei thingy?' We sat silent and sad on the beach, and waited and hoped. She turned to me, her eyes brim-full of tears. 'He will come back, won't he?' she said.

'Course he will,' I said. 'And so will Sergei Ivanovitch Prokofiev. After all we lit the light, didn't we?' I wasn't sure which of us I was trying to convince, Polly or myself. Anyway, I didn't think either of us believed me any more.

It was then we spotted something coming out of the heat-haze around the headland, something low and long like a fat floating cigar. We were both on our feet and running down towards the water. 'What is it?' cried Polly. 'What is it?'

'It's a submarine,' I said, 'and it's coming this way.'

As it came closer we could see that there were dozens of men on the deck and up in the conning-tower. The sun was glinting on their binoculars. They were pointing at us and shouting. We stood there and watched as the submarine glided in silently through the shallows and came to a grinding halt in the sand just a few feet away from us. There was more angry shouting and then sailors were climbing down into the sea and wading up the beach towards us. Until that moment I had never even thought of running. Now suddenly when I did, it was too late.

The first to reach us was a tall bearded man in a blue uniform and a peaked cap. He frowned down at us for a moment and then he saluted. 'Good morning,' he said. 'I am Kapitan Sergei Ivanovitch Prokofiev.'

Polly was beaming at him. 'We know,' she said. 'And you're Russian aren't you?' The captain looked a little surprised.

'Da, da,' he said, and he went on in halting English: 'My ship, she is not so good. Her rudder is, how you say it? Kaput.'

'Busted,' said Polly. 'Your rudder is busted.'

'Busted,' said Sergei Ivanovitch Prokofiev and as he smiled through his black beard, I noticed that his eyebrows met in the middle. 'My sailors, they will make her better and soon we shall be gone again.' He looked around him at the rocks. 'We were lucky, very lucky,' he said. 'All night we cannot steer my ship. Then we see this strange light and the rudder she take us straight towards it and we can do nothing. And then in the morning we see rocks ahead and I think my ship she will soon be . . .

how you say it? Busted? But the rudder she has her own ideas, and she changed course and we find this nice sandy beach to land on, and two nice children to welcome us. My rudder she may be busted, but she's a pretty all right rudder just the same. My engineers they make it better. One hour they say, maybe two.'

'You want a cup of tea?' said Polly. It was more a command than an invitation. 'We got tea in the house and we got Welsh cakes too, haven't we, Mikey? You like Welsh cakes, don't you?'

It was all going to happen just like Dadci said. She was going to make it happen. She went right up to the Russian captain and took his hand. There were sailors all around us now, dozens of them. 'They can come too,' Polly said. 'I want you to meet Dadci and Mum and Da, and Barry too – he's my brother. I specially want you to meet Barry 'cos he never believed you'd come, see.' I have to say I was looking forward to that too. I couldn't wait to see the look on his face. All the way back along the cliff path I tried to swallow the giggle in my throat.

The Russian sailors trooped along behind us laughing and joking. Well, I think they were joking, but of course I couldn't understand a word they were saying. Then they started trying out their English on us. One of them came up alongside me and ruffled my hair. All he could say was: 'Liverpool, good eh? Tottenham Hotspur, good?' I tried to tell him I didn't like football much, but I don't think he understood me. So I tried the only Russian words I'd picked up. 'Da, da,' I said. 'Vodka, vodka.' And I had forty Russian sailors cheering and laughing lustily as we came at last into the farmyard.

Aunty Eleri must have heard us coming.

She came running out of the house, her hands white with flour. Dadci put his head out of the bathroom window. Half his face was covered with shaving soap.

'Mum,' said Polly. 'This is Captain Sergei Ivanovitch . . . Thingy.'

'Prokofiev,' I said.

'It's him, Dadci,' she went on. 'Honest it is.' She turned to the Russian captain. 'You are, aren't you?' she said.

The captain saluted and smiled. 'Da, da. Kapitan Sergei Ivanovitch Prokofiev,' he said. 'And these are my men. My ship she is . . . busted.'

'What?' said Aunty Eleri who had turned about as white as her flour.

'Busted,' said the Russian captain. 'But soon she will be all right and all better again.'

I could see Dadci wiping the soap off his face and then he shook his head very slowly.

'Jumping Jehosophats,' he said, and that was all he said.

'They've come for tea,' said Polly. 'I said they could.'

'There we are then,' said Aunty Eleri, more her old self now as she shook the captain's hand. 'You're all of you very welcome. I'll bring out the tea just as soon as I've boiled a kettle. Give us a hand, Polly, will you?'

'Where's Barry, Mum?' she said as she followed Aunty Eleri indoors.

'Still at the doctor's with Da,' said Aunty Eleri. 'He'll be back soon.'

'I hope so,' said Polly. And so did I.

We had tea in the front garden around the swing, and there were just enough Welsh cakes to go round if we all had just half a one each. 'If I'd known I'd have made some sandwiches,' said Aunty Eleri apologetically, 'but I've run right out of bread. Polly,' she said, 'put the kettle on again will you?' I loved it when she said that. Polly put the kettle on at least six times. The Russian sailors were drinking out of cups, mugs, cereal bowls, sugar bowls, milk jugs, anything we could find. Dadci kept shaking his head and muttering into his tea.

Sitting in Uncle Rob's stripey deckchair Captain Sergei Ivanovitch Prokofiev said how much they all liked the Welsh cakes. He was quite a cook himself he said and he'd like to know how to make them so he could make them back home. And then he sighed a little sadly I thought and put his mug down on the grass. 'I am lucky man,' he said. 'I shall soon be going back home, not like my poor grandfather. I am called after my grandfather you know, the same name, Sergei Ivanovitch Prokofiev, and he was captain of ship too, not submarine of course. He had great big sailing ship – very beautiful, very big, very fast, fastest ship in Russia. I have seen pictures. It is sad story to tell. His ship she goes down in big, big storm – off coast of Wales, maybe not far from here, I think. Everyone they are drowned except my grandfather and ship's boy. Ship's boy he come home alone a year later, maybe two; and he say how my grandfather is alive but he will never come home to Russia. He is full of shame because he has lost his men and his ship. So he say to ship's boy he will never go to sea again. He will become lighthouse keeper somewhere so he can stop ships from coming on to rocks. And so my grandmother she never see him no more. But when she is old she has tame seagull with bad leg, and she say to everyone that the seagull is her Sergei Ivanovitch come back to her at last, and she is happy. Some people, they think she is mad because she is old; but I think it is true maybe.'

'It's true all right,' said Dadci, almost to himself. 'It's true.'

A hooter sounded in the distance and the captain got to his feet. 'My ship she is better now I think.' But Dadci would not let them go until he'd taken several photographs. 'Just so we know it really happened,' he said. 'Rob won't believe us else, and nor will Barry.'

Until the very last moment I was hoping against hope that Barry and Uncle Rob would come back in time, but they didn't. We all of us walked back down to the beach with the Russian sailors, and as we went they tried to teach me the names of Russian football teams. They all had wonderful names, but I only remember one: Dynamo Kiev I think it was. Down on the beach the captain said how we must visit him and his family one day and he'd make us some Russian tea and cook us Welsh cakes. 'There we are then,' said Aunty Eleri shaking his hand. 'I hope your rudder's better now.'

'She is much better,' he said. 'She is, how you say it, not busted no more.'

Goodbyes were sad, but swiftly over, and then they were all back on board. The engines roared into life and the sea churned around the stern of the submarine. But it did not move. The sailors were looking anxiously over the side and I could see Captain Sergei Ivanovitch Prokofiev leaning out of his conning-tower and he did not look at all pleased. The engines thundered, the submarine shook from end to end and the sea boiled all around. But still the submarine would not move.

'It's stuck fast,' said Dadci, 'and the tide's turning. I'm telling you, if we can't get her off before the tide goes down, then she'll break her back on the sandbank.' Again the engines roared, but the captain was shaking his head.

He took off his cap and wiped his brow with the back of his hand. The submarine's engines fell silent. It was then that I noticed that all the sailors were looking in one direction. I thought at first that maybe they were looking at me. Then I saw that their mouths were wide open and they were staring. You know how you feel sometimes that perhaps there's someone right behind you. I turned to look. The Sandman towered a few feet away from us, and there was bladderwrack hanging down over his arms.

'Oh hello, Mr Sandman,' said Polly brightly. 'This is my mum and this is Dadci. He's the one I told you about, the one that made you up.'

'Jumping Jehosophats,' said Dadci and he sat down with a bump on the rock. Aunty Eleri swallowed hard and sat down beside him. 'Oh dear,' she said. 'Oh dear, oh dear.'

CHAPTER FOUR

'WELL NOW,' SAID THE SANDMAN HITCHING his seaweed belt up over his belly. 'Isn't this a turn up! I go off to find meself some nice fresh bladderwrack for me breakfast, and what do I find when I get back? There's a beach full of people and a great grey cucumber thing lying in the sea and lots of funny fellows gawping at me like I'm maybe an ogre or something.'

'It's not a cucumber,' said Polly. 'It's a ship.'

'A submarine,' I explained.

'A ship!' The Sandman roared with laughter. 'Do you call that a ship?'

'It's a kind of ship,' I said. 'It can go on the water or under the water, whatever it likes.'

'And it's Russian,' Polly went on. 'And you see that man jumping down into the water, he's the captain.'

'And it's stuck,' I said. 'It's going to need a push.'

'Is that so?' said the Sandman thoughtfully. He'd stopped laughing now and was looking far out to sea as the Russian captain waded towards us. I could feel the shadow as he bent over me and whispered. 'Are you certain sure that thing's a ship and not a cucumber at all?'

'Quite sure,' I said.

Captain Sergei Ivanovitch Prokofiev kept his distance from the Sandman, which was hardly surprising I suppose. I introduced them to each other because no one else did and when the captain saluted, the Sandman put his bladder-wrack down on the rock and saluted right back.

'Well, I've never in me life set eyes on such a ship,' said the Sandman to the captain. 'Are you sure she's a floating sort of a ship?'

'Of course,' replied the captain stiffly, 'but first I must get her off the sand. My engines, they try very hard but they cannot pull her off. I do not know what more I can do.'

'Supposing,' said the Sandman, 'just supposing we could somehow push her off, and just supposing she was pointing in the right direction, d'you think she might float all the way over to Ireland maybe?'

'My ship she float anywhere you like,' said the captain. 'My ship, she can go all around the world, but if she stay like she is she will pretty soon be – how you say it, Polly?'

'Busted,' said Polly. 'That's what Dadci said too, didn't you, Dadci?'

'We've got to get her off and quick,' said

Dadci, who seemed to have recovered a bit by then.

'What about the big tractor?' said Aunty Eleri. 'Won't that do?'

'Tractor won't touch it,' said Dadci, shaking his head, 'not in a million years. There's only one way you're going to shift it. You'll need something pulling her, something pushing her, and her engines on full power. Only way.'

The Sandman was smiling broadly now. 'Well now,' he said, 'if that isn't a coincidence. I was just thinking the same thing.' And he put two fingers in his mouth and whistled. Gulls, fulmars, shags and cormorants shrieked in alarm and lifted off the cliffs all around us. 'Come on in, boys,' cried the Sandman, and he whistled again, even louder this time.

Out in the bay beyond the submarine, the three giant turtles bobbed up one after the other. 'There's your pullers,' said the Sandman.

'All we need now is three good strong ropes. Would you be having such a thing, captain, down in your cucumber somewhere?' Captain Sergei Ivanovitch Prokofiev was looking rather bewildered, but he nodded. 'Good,' said the Sandman, 'and I'll be the pusher.'

'You?' The captain laughed. 'You will push and turtles will pull?'

'Isn't that a grand idea?' said the Sandman and he was smiling from ear to ear.

'But my ship, she is big, she is heavy. Is not possible,' said the captain.

The Sandman said nothing, but turned to Dadci and Aunty Eleri. 'If you don't mind, I'll be needing that rock you're sitting on.' Dadci and Aunty Eleri stood up and moved away. 'Of course, I haven't had me breakfast yet,' said the Sandman breathing in and out through his teeth and flexing his fingers, 'but let's see what I can do all the same.' And with that he bent down and slipped his arms under the rock. He lifted it to shoulder height and then, balancing it on the palm of one hand, he tossed it over the submarine and out into the sea beyond, where it landed with a great showering splash. All of us looked at each other for a moment.

'See?' said Polly proudly.

'Jumping Jehosophats!' said Dadci.

The Sandman looked very pleased with himself. 'It's like this,' he said. 'Me and the boys – that's me darlin' turtles out there – we'd be happy to help you out; but it's like me old mother always said, "you scratch my back and I'll scratch yours," if you see what I'm saying.' You could tell from the look on his face that Captain Sergei Ivanovitch Prokofiev hadn't a clue what the Sandman meant. 'Well, how shall I put it?' said the Sandman. 'Will you take a look out there? That's me poor old coracle that brought me over from Ireland, and it's all upside-downed and no use at all any more. So I was wondering maybe if I was to give you a little push and me boys out there were to give you a little pull, then maybe you could take me back home to Ireland in your cucumber. What do you say now?'

The captain thought for a moment scratching his beard. Then he shook his head. 'Is not possible,' he said. 'My ship she is too small. You are too big to go inside.'

'Sure that's just a little thing,' said the Sandman. 'I'll sit on top, so I will. I'll ride your cucumber all the way back home. Well?'

The Russian captain seemed a little happier with that. 'Da, da,' he said. 'All right. We try it.'

'But you got to give him lots of food,' said Polly, 'else he'll go to sleep and then he'll fall off. He likes bladderwrack sandwiches. That's seaweed.'

'If he push my ship off the sand,' said the

captain, 'then I promise you I give him all the seaweed sandwiches he want.'

It took a little time to get the turtles ready. First they had to have their milk and soggy crusts and then they had to be roped up. Meanwhile the Sandman asked for his breakfast and so Polly made up the sandwiches. He settled down on the sand and stuffed himself with crunchy bladderwrack sandwiches, and then he emptied the churn of milk down his throat. I waited for his burp, and when it came it was just as loud and long as I'd hoped for; and when Polly giggled we all did, including Aunty Eleri, and that surprised me.

The Sandman stood up. 'Well, I'd better be on me way then,' he said, and he thanked us all and promised he'd come back and see us sometime. And Polly gave him her tooth that had fallen out in the night.

'For luck,' she said, and he scooped her up and kissed her on the cheek.

'Aren't you the darlin' girl?' he said, and he set her down again beside me. He winked at me and said, 'I'll be seeing you.' Then he whistled to the turtles to take the strain and the engines started up. He splashed out through the shallows to the submarine, spat on his hands, took a deep breath and began to push. Nothing moved. He pushed again, harder this time, blowing his cheeks into great balloons. On board the Russian sailors looked down over the sides and shook their heads. The sea churned, the turtles paddled, the Sandman huffed and puffed, and still the submarine would not shift.

'Come on, boys,' he bellowed, but I could see the turtles could do no more than they were doing.

'Gee up! Gee up!' cried Polly, and she was

jumping up and down and cheering them on. Then the Sandman was calling for us to help, and we all of us ran down into the water and threw ourselves against the hull of the submarine. Polly arrived last because she'd tripped over; and I swear the moment she touched that submarine it moved. And then I saw the Sandman's face. He was smiling down at me.

'Oh she's terrible strong, that girl,' he said. 'Who'd have thought it? She's gone and done it all by herself.' You could see Polly believed every word he said, and I knew then, we'd never hear the last of it.

As the submarine inched away seaward the sailors cheered, and then she was free of the sand and the Sandman vaulted on board. The rest of us went on pushing until the sea was too deep for us to go any further; and by this time the Sandman was sitting astride the

bow and waving back at us, and Captain Sergei Ivanovitch Prokofiev took off his hat and led his crew in three ringing Russian hoorahs, and they were all for us. 'Shivery,' said Polly, and I knew what she meant. Aunty Eleri thought she meant something else and rushed her back out of the water before she caught a chill. By the time we reached the cliff path, the submarine was already way out beyond Coracle Rock, the three giant turtles still out in front, and across

the water I was almost sure I could hear singing. Perhaps it was the Sandman or perhaps it was the Russian sailors. Maybe it was both.

We'd all had hot baths and were sitting drying our hair in the kitchen when we heard Uncle Rob's car draw up outside. 'Who's going to tell them then?' said Aunty Eleri, and we all knew the answer to that.

'Me,' said Polly, and of course she did. They

had hardly set foot inside the door before she started. Aunty Eleri, Dadci and I, we just looked at the floor and listened. 'And I pushed it out all by myself,' Polly said. 'Honest.' She had finished at last. Uncle Rob smiled and patted her head as Barry limped across the room towards me on his crutches.

'I've had my stitches out, Mike,' he said, pointing to his forehead and ignoring Polly completely.

'But it's true,' Polly cried. 'Cross my heart.'

'Here, my stitches. I kept them,' said Barry, and he handed me a little envelope. 'Doctor gave them to me.' There were bits of dark cotton inside. Bit disgusting I thought.

'No concussion,' said Uncle Rob. 'Doctor says he can do what he likes. Plaster comes off in six weeks.'

'There you are then,' said Aunty Eleri. 'That's nice.'

Barry was standing right in front of me. 'What's happened to you then?'

I shrugged my shoulders. 'I got wet,' I said.

'Pushing out the Russian submarine, I suppose?' said Barry.

'Yes,' I said, but I didn't dare look him in the face.

'That's quite a story, Polly,' said Uncle Rob. 'You get better and better. For just a moment there you had me half believing you.'

And then Aunty Eleri spoke up. 'I know this is hard to believe,' she said, 'but I'm afraid it's all quite true, everything Polly said, every word of it.' Uncle Rob and Barry tried to laugh it off at first. Then for some time no one said anything. You could hear the kitchen clock ticking loudly in the silence.

'Don't be a cuckoo,' said Uncle Rob. 'Fair play now.'

'True as I'm sitting here,' said Dadci.

'Everything. The Sandman, the turtles and the submarine. And Captain Sergei Ivanovitch Prokofiev – he's the lighthouse keeper's grandson, just like Polly said. I took some photos. True now.'

'What is this?' said Uncle Rob. 'An April Fool in August?'

'Mike?' said Barry, and this time I had to look at him.

'Well . . .' I said, trying to find the words.

'Lot of rot,' said Uncle Rob, and there was an edge to his voice now. 'Stories is stories, but that's all they are. You shouldn't go encouraging her like that.'

'But, Rob,' Aunty Eleri tried to interrupt him, and so did Dadci, and so did Polly. Uncle Rob would have none of it.

'A joke's a joke,' he said firmly, 'and this one's not funny any more.' Polly went on protesting and then Uncle Rob got really angry.

'I don't want to hear any more about it, understand? Now I've got work to do. There's a fence down above Whaletooth Beach. I'll take the tractor. You coming, Barry?'

'Yes, I'm coming,' said Barry, and I could hear the cold anger in him. 'Load of rubbish,' he muttered as he limped out after Uncle Rob.

'Pegleg!' Polly shouted after him and she turned to Aunty Eleri. 'They don't believe us, Mum. Why won't they believe us?' Her eyes were filled with tears.

'Don't you worry, Polly,' said Aunty Eleri putting her arm round her. 'They'll believe us when the photos come out. They'll have to, won't they, Dadci?'

Dadci was taking the camera down off the mantelpiece. He turned around. 'I'm afraid there won't be any photos,' he said. 'I just remembered, there's no film in it.'

Uncle Rob and Barry never came back for

lunch, and I was upstairs in the bathroom reading one of Barry's Tintin books, the one about the yetis, when I heard the tractor come rattling into the yard. There were footsteps running across the cobbles, and then Uncle Rob was calling excitedly. 'Quickly!' he shouted. 'Come quick!' I pulled up my trousers and ran downstairs taking the steps two at a time, still doing up my zip. Not easy that. As I came through the sitting-room I caught a glimpse through the window of Aunty Eleri and Polly and Dadci haring out across the fields towards the cliffs. Beyond them there was a column of black smoke rising into the sky. Uncle Rob came in then doubled up with laughter, and Barry behind him giggling like I'd never seen him. Uncle Rob helped Barry down on to the sofa and then collapsed into his armchair. They were both howling uncontrollably.

'You been burning off the bracken?' I asked,

but neither of them was capable of replying. 'What's going on?' I said. I was beginning to feel a little left out and I didn't much like it.

'We fixed 'em,' said Barry, and they managed between fits of rib-aching laughter to tell me all about it. 'We fixed 'em good, didn't we, Da?'

'We did,' said Uncle Rob still wheezing. 'We did indeed – with a little help from the dragon of course, y'know the blood-red one, the spikey one. Funny thing though, not a sign of the dragon was there? And we looked everywhere didn't we? Knocked on his door and he never came out.' And they were both heaving again. 'We thought, didn't we, Barry, we thought maybe he'd gone shopping.'

Barry went on when he could. 'You'll never guess what we did. We made this pile of driftwood, didn't we, Da? And then Da poured on the diesel, and then we threw on a couple of old tyres from the silage pit.'

'Blackens the smoke something terrific that does,' said Uncle Rob.

'Dragons make black smoke, remember?' said Barry. 'Just like Dadci says they do. Then we get back here as quick as we can and we tell 'em. You tell it like you told 'em, Da. Da was brilliant, Mike, you should have seen him.'

Uncle Rob was on his feet and pointing. ' "Quick," I said. "Down on Whaletooth," I said. "We was down there fencing, the two of us; and Barry here, he chucks a stone into a cave. He didn't mean any harm, did you, Barry? And a moment later there's this roaring and then there's this thick black smoke billowing out of the cave. Never seen nothing like it. And then out comes this spikey blood-red dragon belching fire and smoke. Well we didn't hang about I can tell you. Last we saw of him, he was coming up through the bracken

and half the hillside was on fire. Hurry now." I
told them. But I needn't have. I've never seen
Dadci move so fast. Going like the clappers he
was when I last saw him; and Polly was all
leaping up and down and screaming, "The
dragon's true too, the dragon's true too." ' And
he sat down again groaning with laughter and
wiping the tears from his eyes.

'Good one, eh, Mike?' said Barry. 'Good as
any daft Russian submarine?'

But I had heard something outside. I was
looking out of the window. Polly was running
back across the fields looking over her shoulder
and falling over herself all the time; and then I
saw Aunty Eleri dragging Dadci along by his
hand. They were in a hurry too. And as I
watched I saw a spikey blood-red dragon come
lurruping along behind them breathing out
orange flames and black smoke and setting fire
to the bracken as it came. I didn't know quite

what to say. Well, I didn't want to sound stupid – you can understand that can't you? So looking them straight in the eye and with my voice as calm as I could make it I just said: 'You're not going to believe this.'